BARRON'S

Princess Penny
and her
dancing sister!

This book belongs to a princess named

This is Princess Penny.

This is Princess Polly.

They are **sisters,** and they love spending time together.
They each have a bedroom at the top of a tower in a
huge castle on the edge of the forest.

They love exploring the kingdom on their ponies and discovering new places, which can sometimes get them into BIG trouble!

On sunny days they enjoy chasing **butterflies** in the castle gardens.

But their favorite way of keeping busy is **dancing!**

Whenever they hear music, their fingers start **clicking,**
their toes start **tapping,** and they start to **dance!**

Sometimes they practice **ballroom** dancing . . .

Sometimes they try **ballet** dancing . . .

And sometimes they even try **break dancing!**

There was only **one thing** that spoiled their fun . . .

It didn't matter how hard she tried—Princess Penny could not dance like Princess Polly!

When they pirouetted, she always **fell over!**
When they waltzed, she stood on Princess Polly's **toes!**
And when they break danced, she would always **break things!**

One bright Monday morning, the princesses had just finished grooming
their ponies when an enormous, brightly colored butterfly
fluttered across the stable yard.

Princess Polly and Princess Penny could not resist chasing it. But soon they were deep in the forest . . .

Eventually, they stopped on the edge of a stream, and as they rested, the sound of **music** drifted through the trees.

Immediately, their fingers started **clicking**, their toes started **tapping**, and they found themselves **dancing** and **twirling** toward the music.

They followed the twisty path through the trees, where they discovered the music was coming through the windows of a **crooked cottage.**

Lying on the path in front of the cottage was a ladder,
and sitting next to it was a large gray and white cat.

The princesses danced into the garden, where Polly performed a **perfect twirl.**

But poor Penny tripped over her feet and landed in a **rosebush!** Ouch!

As she lay there, she looked up at the cottage, and to her amazement there was a little old lady sitting on the roof!

The princesses rushed to put the ladder back up, and the old lady climbed down. She told them she had been rescuing her cat, but he had jumped down, knocking the ladder over and leaving her **stuck!**

"I don't know how to thank you! I don't have much money for a reward, so perhaps I could give you one of my **gold cups**. I won them for **dancing** when I was young."

"I know!" shouted Princess Polly excitedly. "You can help Penny with her dancing, and then she won't break things anymore!"

And that is exactly what happened!
Every day the old lady taught Princess Penny until she was
spinning and twirling just as beautifully as Princess Polly!